A BANANA BOOK

CONKER

Michael Morpurgo

Illustrated by
LINDA BIRCH

HEINEMANN · LONDON

Reprinted 1989, 1992, 1993
Text © 1987 Michael Morpurgo
Illustrations © 1987 Linda Birch
ISBN 0 434 93044 X

A school pack of BANANAS 19-24 is
available from Heinemann Educational Books
ISBN 0 435 00103 5

A CIP catalogue record for this book is
available at the British Library

Printed in Italy by Olivotto

MOST DOGS HAVE one name, but
Pooch had three – one after the other.
Pooch was what Grandma called him in
the first place. But when Nick was a
toddler he couldn't say Pooch very well
and so Pooch soon became Pooh.

Then one day Pooh heard the rattle
of the milk bottles outside and came

1

bounding out of the house to say hello to the milkman – he liked the milkman. But today it was a different one. Pooh prowled around him sniffing at the bottom of his trousers. The new milkman went as white as his milk. Nick tried to drag Pooh back into the house, but he wouldn't come.

'S'like a wolf,' said the milkman, putting his hands on his head and backing down the path. 'You ought to chain it up.'

'Not a wolf,' Nick said. 'He's an old station.'

'A what?' said the milkman.

'An old station,' Nick said. 'Pooh is an old station.' At that moment Grandma came to the door.

'Nick gets his words muddled sometimes,' she said. 'He's only little. I think he means an *Alsatian*, don't you

dear? Old Station! Old Station! You are
a funny boy, Nick.' And she laughed so
much that she nearly cried. So from
that day Pooh was called Old Station.

There were always just the three of
them in the house. Nick had lived with
Grandma for as long as he could
remember. She looked after Nick and
Old Station looked after them both.
Everywhere they went Old Station
went with them. 'Don't know what
we'd do without him,' Grandma would
say.

All his life Old Station had been like a big brother to Nick. Nick was nine years old now. He had watched Old Station grow old as he grew up. The old dog moved slowly these days, and when he got up in the morning to go outside you could see it was a real effort. He would spend most of the day asleep in his basket, dreaming his dreams.

Nick watched him that morning as he ate his cornflakes before he went off to school. It was the last day before half-term. Old Station was growling in his sleep as he often did and his whiskers were twitching.

'He's chasing cats in his dreams,' said Grandma. 'Hurry up, Nick, else you'll be late.' She gave him his satchel and packed lunch, and Nick called out 'Goodbye' to Old Station and ran off down the road.

It was a windy autumn morning with the leaves falling all around him. Before he got to school he caught twenty-six of them in mid-air and that was more than he'd ever caught before. By the end of the day the leaves were piled as high as his ankles in the gutters, and Nick scuffled through them on the way back home, thinking of all the bike rides he could go on now that half-term had begun.

Old Station wasn't there to meet h

at the door as he sometimes was, and Grandma wasn't in the kitchen cooking tea as she usually was. Old Station wasn't in his basket either.

Nick found Grandma in the back garden, taking the washing off the line. 'Nice windy day. Wanted to leave the washing out as long as possible,' she said from behind a sheet. 'I'll get your tea in a minute, dear.'

'Where's Old Station?' Nick said.

'... not in his basket.'

Grandma didn't reply, not at first anyway; and when she did Nick wished she never had done.

'He had to go,' Grandma said simply, and she walked past him without even looking at him.

'Go where?' Nick asked. 'What do you mean? Where's he gone to?'

Grandma put the washing down on the kitchen table and sat down heavily in the chair. Nick could see then that she'd been crying, and he knew that Old Station was dead. 'The Vet said he was suffering,' she said, looking up at him. 'We couldn't have him suffering, could we? It had to be done. That's all there is to it. Just a pinprick it was, dear, and then he went off to sleep. Nice and peaceful.'

'He's dead then,' Nick said.

Grandma nodded. 'I buried him

outside in the garden by the wall. It's what was best for him Nick,' she said. 'You know that don't you?' Nick nodded and they cried quietly together.

After tea Grandma put Old Station's basket out in the shed and showed Nick where she had buried him. 'We'll plant something over him, shall we, dear?' she said. 'A rose perhaps, so we won't forget him.'

'We'll never forget him,' said Nick. 'Never.'

The day after Old Station died was Saturday. Saturdays and Sundays in the conker season meant conkers in Jubilee Park with his friends, but Nick didn't feel like seeing anyone, not that day. Every time he looked out of the kitchen window into the back garden he felt like crying. It was Grandma's idea that he should go for a long ride, and so he did. The next best thing in the world after Old Station was the bike Grandma had given him on his birthday. It was shining royal blue with three-speed gears, a bell, a front light and everything. Just to sit on it made him feel happy. By the time he got back from his ride he felt a lot better.

The next morning Nick went off to Jubilee Park as he always did on a Sunday. All his friends were there, and so was Stevie Rooster. Stevie Rooster called himself the "Conker King of Jubilee Park". He was one of those bragging brutish boys who could hit harder, run faster and shout louder than anyone else. There was only one thing Stevie had ever been frightened of, and that was Old Station. Perhaps it was because of Old Station that Nick was the one boy he had never bullied.

Of course they all knew about Old Station, but no one said anything about him, except for Stevie Rooster. 'So that smelly old dog of yours kicked the bucket at last,' he said. Perhaps he was expecting everyone to laugh, but no one did.

Nick tried to stop himself from crying.

Stevie went on, ''Bout time if you ask me.'

In his fury Nick tore the conker out of Stevie Rooster's hand and hurled it into the pond.

'That's my twenty-fiver,' Stevie bellowed, and he lashed out at Nick with his fist, catching him in the mouth.

Nick looked at the blood on the back of his hand and flew at Stevie's throat like an alley cat. In the end Nick was left with a split lip, a black eye and a torn shirt. He was lucky to get away with just that. If the Park Keeper had not come along when he did it might have been a lot worse.

Grandma shook her head as she bathed his face in the kitchen. 'What does it matter what Stevie Rooster says about Old Station?' she said. 'Look what he's done to you. Look at your face.'

'I had to get him,' Nick said.

'But you didn't, did you? I mean he's bigger than you isn't he? He's twice your size and nasty with it. If you want to beat him, you've got to use your head. It's the only way.'

'What do you mean, Grandma?' Nick asked. 'What else could I do?'

'Conkers,' said Grandma. 'Didn't you tell me once that he likes to call himself the "Conker King of Jubilee Park"?'

'Yes.'

'Well then,' said Grandma. 'You've got to knock him off his throne, haven't you?'

'But how?'

'You've got to beat him at conkers,' she said. 'And I'm going to teach you how. There's nothing I don't know about conkers, Nick, nothing. You'll see.'

Somehow Nick had never thought of his Grandma as a conker expert.

'First we must find the right conkers,' she went on. 'And there's

only one place to find a champion
conker and that's from the old conker
tree out by Cotter's Yard. It's still
standing, I saw it from the bus only the
other day. I never had a conker off that
tree that let me down. Always hard as
nails they are. Mustn't be any bigger
than my thumbnail. Small and hard is
what we're after.'

And so it was that Nick found
himself that afternoon cycling along the
road out of town, past the football
ground and the gasworks, with a packet
of jelly babies in his pocket. 'Now don't
eat them all at once, dear,' Grandma
had told him. 'Go carefully and look for
the tree on the left-hand side of the
road just as you come to Cotter's Yard;
you know, the scrapyard where they
crunch up old cars. You can't miss it.'
And Grandma's conker tree was just

where she said it was, a great towering conker tree standing on its own by the scrapyard.

Nick must have spent half an hour searching through the leaves under the tree, but he couldn't find a single conker. He was about to give up and go home when he spotted a cluster of

prickly green balls lying in the long
grass on the other side of the fence.
There was no sign of life in Cotter's
Yard. No one would be there on a
Sunday afternoon. No one would mind
if he went in just to pick up conkers.
There was nothing wrong with that he
thought.

He climbed quickly. At the top he swung his legs over and dropped down easily on the other side. He found the cluster of three small conkers and broke them open. Each one was shining brown and perfect, and just the right size. He stuffed them into his pocket and was just about to climb out again when he heard from somewhere behind him in Cotter's Yard, the distant howling of a dog. His first thought was to scramble up over the fence and escape, but then the howling stopped and the dog began to whine and whimper and yelp. It was a cry for help which Nick could not ignore.

Cotter's Yard was a maze of twisted rusting wrecks. The muddy tracks through it were littered with car tyres. Great piles of cars towered all about him now as he picked his way round the potholes. And all the while the pitiful howling echoed louder around him. He was getting closer.

He found the guard dog sitting by a hut in the centre of the Yard. He was chained by the neck to a metal stake, and he was shivering so much that his teeth were rattling. The chain was twisted over his back and wrapped round his back legs so that he could

not move. 'Doesn't look ferocious,'
Nick thought, 'but you never know.'
And he walked slowly around the guard
dog at a safe distance.

And then Nick noticed the dog's face.
It was as if Old Station had come back
from the grave and was looking up at
him. He had the same gentle brown
eyes, the same way of holding his head

23

on one side when he was thinking. Old
Station liked jelly babies, Nick thought.
Perhaps this one will. One by one the
dog took them gently out of Nick's
hand, chewed them, swallowed them
and then waited for the next one.
When there were no more Nick gave
him the paper bag to play with whilst

he freed him from the chain. He ate
the bag too, and when he stood up and
shook himself, Nick could see that he
was thin like a greyhound is thin.
There were sores around his neck
behind his ears where his collar had
rubbed him raw.

Nick sat down beside him, took off his duffle coat and rubbed him and rubbed him until his teeth stopped chattering. He didn't like to leave him, but it was getting dark. 'Don't worry,' Nick said, walking away. The dog followed him to the end of his chain. 'I'll be back,' he said. 'I promise I will.' Nick knew now exactly what he wanted to do, but he had no idea at all how he was going to do it.

It was dark by the time Nick got home and Grandma was not pleased with him. 'Where have you been? I was worried sick about you,' she said, taking off his coat and shaking it out.

'The conkers were difficult to find, Grandma,' Nick said, but he said no more.

Grandma was pleased with the conkers though. 'Just like they always were,' she said, turning them over in her hands. 'Unbreakable little beauties.' And then Grandma began what she called her 'conker magic'. First she put them in the oven for exactly twelve minutes. Then she took them out and dropped them still hot into a pudding basin full of her conker potion, a mixture of vinegar, salt, mustard and a teaspoon of Worcester Sauce. One hour

later she took them out again and put
them back into the oven for another
twelve minutes. When they came out
they were dull and crinkled. She
polished them with furniture polish till
they shone again. Then she drove a
small brass nail through the conkers
one after the other and examined each
one carefully. She put two of them
aside and held up the third in triumph

'This is the one,' she said. 'This is your champion conker. All you have to do now, Nick, is sleep with that down the bottom of your bed tonight and tomorrow you'll be Conker King of Jubilee Park.'

But Nick couldn't sleep that night. He lay there thinking of the dog he had left behind in Cotter's Yard, and about how he was going to rescue him. By breakfast the next morning he was still not sure how to set about it.

'Remember, you must play on a short string,' Grandma was saying.

'And always play on grass so it won't break if he pulls it out of your hand. And try not to get tangled up – puts a strain on the knot. What's the matter with you, dear? You're not eating your breakfast.'

'Grandma,' Nick said, 'what if you found a dog all chained up and lonely and miserable, would you try to rescue it?'

'What makes you ask a thing like that, dear?' Grandma said.

'Would you?' Nick asked.

'Of course, dear.'

'Even if it meant stealing it, Grandma?'

'Ah well, that's different. Two wrongs don't make a right, Nick,' she said. 'What's all this about?'

'Oh nothing, nothing,' Nick said quickly. 'I was just thinking, that's all.'

Nick could feel she was suspicious. He had said far too much already. He left quickly before she could ask any more questions.

'Good luck, Nick,' Grandma called after him as he went off down the path.

He cycled right up to Stevie Rooster in the Park and challenged him there and then. 'I've got a conker that'll beat any conker you've got,' he said. Stevie

31

Rooster laughed at Nick and his little
conker, but when his first conker broke
in two the smile left his face. He took
conker after conker out of his sack, and
each one was shattered into little pieces
within seconds. A crowd gathered as
Nick's conker became a twentier, a
thirtier, a fiftier and then at last an
eighty-fiver. Stevie Rooster's face was

red with fury as he took his last conker
out of his sack.

'Your turn,' Nick said quietly and he
held up his conker. There still wasn't a
mark on it. Stevie swung again and was
left holding a piece of empty string
with a knot swinging at the end of it.
Nick looked him in the face and saw
the tears of humiliation start into his
eyes. 'You shouldn't have said that
about Old Station,' Nick said and he

turned, got on his bike and cycled off leaving a stunned crowd behind him.

It was a twenty minute ride up to Cotter's Yard, but Nick did it in ten. All through the conker game he had been thinking about it and now at last he knew what to do. He had a plan. He was breathless by the time he got there. The gates were wide open. The Yard was working today, the great crane swinging out over the crushing machine, a car hanging from its jaws.

'Hey you, what're you after?' It was a voice from the door of the hut. It belonged to a weasel-faced man with mean little eyes.

'I've come to buy your dog,' Nick said. 'Haven't got any money, but I'll swop my bike for your dog. It's almost new, three speed and everything. Had it for my birthday, a month ago.' Nick looked around for the dog, but there was no sign of him. The chain lay curled up in the mud by the hut.

'Haven't got no dog here,' said the weasel-faced man, 'not any more. Wasn't any use anyway. Got rid of him, didn't I?'

'What do you mean?' Nick said.

'Just what I said. I got rid of him. Vet came and took him away this morning. No use to me he wasn't. Now push off out of here.' And he went back inside the hut and slammed the door behind him.

As Nick walked home, the rain came spitting down through the trees. He had never felt more miserable in his life. When Old Station died he had been sad enough, but this was different and much, much worse. This had been his fault. If only he had come back earlier, if only. By the time he reached home he was blinded with tears.

'Well, and how's the Conker King of Jubilee Park?' Grandma called out from the kitchen as he closed the door behind him, and she came hurrying out to meet him. 'Well I told you, didn't I?

I told you. It's all down the street.
Everyone knows my Nick's the Conker
King. Well, come on, let's see the
famous conker. An eighty-fiver, isn't
it?'

'Eighty-sixer,' Nick said and burst
into tears against her apron.

'What's all this?' Grandma said,
putting an arm round him and leading
him into the kitchen. 'We can't have
the Conker King of Jubilee Park crying
his eyes out.' And Nick blurted it all
out, all about Cotter's Yard and the
poor starving dog he had found there

that looked just like Old Station, about how the vet had come and taken him away.

'I was going to buy him for you with my bike,' Nick said, 'to take Old Station's place, but I was too late.'

'Who says you were?' said Grandma, and there was a certain tone in her voice.

'What do you mean?' Nick asked.

'What I mean, dear, is that if you'd wipe your eyes and look over in the corner there, you'd see a basket with a dog in it, and if you looked hard at that dog you might just recognise him.'

Nick looked. The dog from Cotter's Yard lay curled up in Old Station's basket, his great brown eyes gazing up at him. The dog got up, stretched, yawned and came over to him.

'But how . . .?' Nick began.

Grandma held up her hand.

'When you came home from Cotter's Yard yesterday with your duffle coat stinking of dog, I was a little suspicious. You see, old Cotter's known for the cruel way he looks after his guard dogs, always has been. And then when you asked me this morning if I would rescue a dog if I found him all chained up and hungry and miserable – well, I put two and two together.'

'But he said the Vet came and took him away – he told me,' Nick said.

'So he did, dear, so he did. We went out there together, the vet and me, and we made old Cotter an offer he couldn't refuse. Either we took his dog with us or we reported him for cruelty to animals. Didn't take him long to make up his mind, I can tell you.'

'So he's ours then, Grandma?' Nick said.

'Yours, Nick, he's yours. Old Station was mine. I had him even before I had you, remember? But this one's yours, your prize for winning the Conker Championship of Jubilee Park. Now can I see that famous conker or can't I?'

Nick fished the conker out of his pocket and held it up by the string. Before he knew it, the dog had jumped up and jerked it out of his hand. A few seconds later all that was left was a mass of wet crumbs and chewed string.

'It looks as if he likes conkers for his tea,' Grandma said.

'Better call him "Conker" then,' Nick said. And so they did.